This book is dedicated to the memory of Angel,
Grasshopper, and Bunny.
These three cats were very special and
taught us many important lessons.

www.mascotbooks.com

Angel and the Butterfly

For more information, please contact:
Mascot Books
620 Herndon Parkway, Suite 320
Herndon, VA 20170
info@mascotbooks.com

Library of Congress Control Number: 2020901258

CPSIA Code: PRT0320A
ISBN-13: 978-1-64543-178-7

Printed in the United States

Angel and the Butterfly

Darlene Mallich

illustrated by Alaina Luise

Angel, Grasshopper, and Bunny were very special, and they taught us many lessons. One of those lessons can be found in the following poem that was inspired by them.

A Bird's Song

Why does a bird's song ring so true,
Its flight impelling our flight too?
Why do they fly so high and free,
To set an example for you and me?

Could they be flying to show us the way?
Or could they simply be trying to say,
"You can fly too, you know that you can,
Just reach up here and give me your hand.

"We'll fly as high as we can reach,
And once you've flown, then you can teach,
Others now that they can, too,
Do anything they want to do."

Angel was a sweet, young Siamese kitten who had the most beautiful blue eyes and velvety soft fur. He always stood out as being the most adorable and inquisitive kitten.

One day, Angel found himself all alone in a beautiful large park. He wandered too far from home and was lost and getting scared. He had never been alone before.

There were lots of trees, flowers, hills, and bushes in the park. Angel wandered around for three days, hiding in the bushes and looking for food. He was confused and was getting very, very hungry. *Now what do I do?* Angel wondered.

Angel looked up. There were lots of butterflies flying around high over his head, so he jumped up and tried to grab one as it flew by.

"Hey!" shouted Butterfly. "You could hurt me with your sharp claws, you know!"

Angel was surprised that Butterfly had spoken to him. He was used to watching butterflies as they danced through the air on sunny days. They looked like they were having so much fun playing games with each other. He often wondered how it must feel to be so light and free. They looked so happy. He used to imagine himself feeling that happy, too.

Maybe Butterfly would know where I can find some food, he thought.

"Oh, Butterfly," Angel sweetly inquired. "You can see much farther from up there than I can from down here. Can you please tell me where I might find some food?"

Angel had a very sweet face, and Butterfly found him to be quite charming.

"Food?" Butterfly responded. "What kind of food? There are many flowers to choose from, and flowers are delicious. Come and see, over this way."

Butterfly led Angel across the park to where there were many flowers of all kinds. There were yellow ones, red ones, purple ones, and orange ones—so many to choose from!

But Angel had never eaten a flower before and wasn't sure what to do. Butterfly, sensing Angel's confusion, landed on a nearby flower to demonstrate.

Angel watched as Butterfly uncurled her long tongue to drink nectar from the flower. "See," said Butterfly as she began sipping nectar from the center of the flower.

I can do that, too, he thought. So, Angel leaned over one of the purple flowers and sniffed it.

Ah-choo! Ah-choo! Ah-choo! he sneezed.

Angel backed away from the flowers, rubbing his eyes with his paws. "Do you actually eat this stuff?" he sniffled.

"Maybe you need something different," Butterfly said. She remembered seeing a cat chase a mouse the other day in the hilly section of the park where the rocks were. "Follow me!" she shouted.

Angel and Butterfly headed off to the other side of the park. Angel was running below as Butterfly flittered playfully overhead. Butterfly looked like she was having so much fun! You could tell by the way she was fluttering her wings and laughing out loud. Butterfly loved to explore, try new things, and, of course, she loved to fly.

Angel could feel the freedom and joy that Butterfly was feeling. "This is it," he shouted. "This is what it feels like to be happy and free!"

Once they arrived at the rocks, Angel saw a sudden movement out of the corner of his eye. He ran to that spot, but a little mouse scurried away into a hole along the side of a large rock, just in time to avoid Angel's pounce.

Angel sat down. He was so disappointed that the mouse had gotten away from him. "I have never had to catch my own food before," Angel sighed. "I am so hungry."

Angel mournfully walked over to a small puddle of water left over from the recent rains. As he sipped from the puddle of water, he imagined himself sleeping on a comfortable, warm pillow on top of a nice, soft bed. "Oh, what is to become of me?" he said.

Just then, Butterfly had another idea.
She remembered seeing two cats the
other day at a house very near the park.
There were lots of pretty flowers in the
yard, and the cats looked so happy there.
Maybe they would know what to do.

Butterfly spoke to Angel about her idea. Angel was so hungry that he was willing to try just about anything. So, they began their journey to the house with the cats in the yard.

When Butterfly and Angel arrived at the backyard, Butterfly gracefully landed on top of the fence that overlooked the yard with the two cats. Angel followed below and peeked through a hole near the bottom of the fence. *Hmmm*, he thought. *This looks like a wonderful place to live.*

"Excuse me, please," Angel said through the fence to the cats. "Do you know where I can get some food?"

Grasshopper—who was older and wiser than his sister, Bunny—looked up from his nap. He saw a nose and two eyes peeking at him through the hole in the fence. "Who's there?!" he demanded.

Angel realized that he needed to get to the other
side of the fence so that Grasshopper could see him.
Angel gracefully leapt in a single motion to the top of
the fence and sat right next to Butterfly.

Grasshopper looked up at Angel. "I don't remember
seeing you around here before," he stated.

Angel replied, "I have been living in the park for three
days without food, and I am very hungry and lonely.
Can you help me?"

Bunny, who had been quietly observing from the side, noticed what a sweet face Angel had and liked him right away. Bunny also remembered seeing Butterfly earlier that week while she had been napping in the yard, and she trusted Butterfly.

Usually Grasshopper and Bunny would just sit in their backyard enjoying the warm sun for hours at a time, licking their fur clean and sometimes playing with little bugs crawling nearby. Bunny, who was much younger than Grasshopper, was excited about the idea of having someone her own age to play with.

Bunny turned to Grasshopper and said, "He looks very nice. Let's invite him in for supper. I'm sure our people will like him, too." Grasshopper agreed.

Grasshopper and Bunny's people opened their hearts to Angel. They fed him, played with him, and loved him. He soon became a special and very important member of their family.

That night, Angel stretched out to sleep on a comfortable, warm pillow on top of a nice, soft bed, just like he had imagined.

Now I understand why I met Butterfly, Angel thought. Their adventure through the park was part of a wonderful journey that led him to his perfect new home. Here he was loved more than he could ever have imagined. Angel had finally learned how to feel free and happy.

"You can fly, too, you know that you can,
Just reach up here and give me your hand."

About the Author

Darlene Mallich spent her entire life loving and caring for animals. As a child, her family had pet dogs, cats, parakeets, pigeons, rabbits, chickens, and ducks. As a young adult, she also had her own horse. Although horses are one of her great loves, the largest part of Darlene's heart belongs to her precious cats.

Darlene's connection with animals throughout her life has been an amazing blessing. Animals of all types are so much more intelligent and sentient than most people realize. She sees animals as our teachers, here to help guide us through life.

Darlene wrote *Angel and the Butterfly* to help demonstrate for young children that they can do anything they want to do. Their only limits are self-imposed. Believing in yourself and following guidance, which comes in many forms, will take you wherever you want to be. She never received that message as a child, so it is important for her to share this with children today.

She hopes you find her story to be uplifting, inspirational, and fun!